SHAKESPEARE FOR EVERYONE

TWELFTH NIGHT

By Jennifer Mulherin   *Illustrations by* George Thompson
CHERRYTREE BOOKS

Author's note

There is no substitute for seeing the plays of Shakespeare performed. Only then can you really understand why Shakespeare is our greatest dramatist and poet. This book simply gives you the background to the play and tells you about the story and characters. It will, I hope, encourage you to see the play.

A Cherrytree Book

Designed and produced by
A S Publishing

First published 1988
by Cherrytree Press Ltd
327 High Street
Slough
Berkshire SL1 1TX

Reprinted 1993, 1995, 1999, 2001

Copyright this edition © Evans Brothers Ltd 2001

British Library Cataloguing in Publication Data
Mulherin, Jennifer
    Twelfth night
    Drama in English. Shakespeare, William
    I. Title II. Thompson, George, 1925-
    III. Series
    822.3'3

ISBN 1 84234 047 6

Printed in Hong Kong through Colorcraft Ltd

Contents

Twelfth Night *and Elizabethan entertainments*

This miniature shows an Elizabethan lady in a masque costume. Masques were rather formal entertainments in which there was singing and dancing. The performers always wore elaborate and beautiful costumes.

Shakespeare's audience would have immediately known, by its title, that his new play *Twelfth Night* was an entertainment. In Elizabethan times, Twelfth Night was the last night of the Christmas holidays and was always celebrated with great merrymaking. There were many feastdays and holidays in the Elizabethan year and ordinary people, as well as the Court, celebrated these in great style.

In those days, Christmas was England's only holiday 'season', and for about two weeks everyone stopped work to enjoy a series of public and private festivities. In towns and villages throughout the land, people made merry until on the 7th January, after the feast of the Epiphany, they returned to work.

The Lord of Misrule

In most villages, as soon as the Christmas holiday began, all the folk gathered together to choose a 'Lord of Misrule'. He was the person who would lead all the merrymaking. He, in turn, chose a group of about 20 followers or more, and together they set about preparing the costumes to wear and the entertainments to be provided for the village.

The revellers always dressed in brightly-coloured garments of red, green or yellow, which were bedecked with scarves, ribbons and lace. They decorated the costumes with rings and jewels and added lots of tiny bells to the legs and arms. Some of these costumes were similar to those worn by court jesters in earlier times – and by the Clown in *Twelfth Night*. When they danced and sang, the bells jingled to the sound of music.

Some of the Lord of Misrule's men played the pipes and drums, others danced popular reels and jigs and there might even be one or two tumblers among the company. The hobby horse or dragon, the body of which was filled with men, was a favourite entertainment. It pranced about the streets, often in front of or behind the dancers, weaving in and out of the crowd and performing antics.

The Master of the Revels

At Court, the preparations for the Christmas festivities were particularly elaborate. They started several weeks before the holiday season began. Elizabeth I had a special Revels Office run by the Master of the Revels. He and his department looked after all Court entertainments right through the year, and there were a great many of these. Not only did the Court celebrate all the feasts and holidays but it also entertained ambassadors and important visitors.

Sometimes, pageants or street processions were arranged but Court revels, especially at Christmas, usually included

This 16th-century Flemish painting shows noblemen hunting deer in the park at Nonsuch Palace. Built in 1540 by Henry VIII, this palace was used by Queen Elizabeth as one of her royal residences.

the performance of a number of plays and one or two masques. We know, for example, that Shakespeare's theatre company performed before the Queen and her Court during the Christmas holidays of 1600-01.

Before a play was selected, the Master of the Revels had to see performances by different theatre companies. He also had to read the plays carefully to make sure that they contained nothing to offend the Queen and her guests. Once a play was agreed upon, the company of actors had to attend rehearsals within the palace, where stage and scenery were different from those in the theatre.

If a masque was to be performed, the Master of the Revels needed to supervise the building of elaborate scenery and costumes. Masques differed from plays: they never told much of a story but were very beautiful to look at, and contained many songs and dances. During the dances, the guests sometimes mingled with the performers (who frequently wore masks) while attendants wearing shimmering costumes carried torches.

Masques were a favourite kind of Court entertainment and although Shakespeare did not write any masques, his friend Ben Jonson did. Many of Ben Jonson's masques were designed by the famous architect, Inigo Jones.

Courtly sports

Not all Court entertainment took place indoors. Queen Elizabeth's favourite sport was hunting and foreign visitors were often taken to a deer hunt. The Queen had her own deer parks filled with stags and does, and many noblemen, like the Duke Orsino in *Twelfth Night*, went hunting. Most ladies watched the deer hunt from afar but the Queen loved to ride with the men, carrying a heavy crossbow with which to shoot the animals.

The performers in masques and similar kinds of Court entertainments were often dressed as imaginary or mythological characters. Great attention was paid to costume design, as well as to scenery.

V.A.M   d· giorgio d'arezzo —   E·614·1936

7

A festive play

In Elizabethan times, it was
fashionable for young
noblemen, like Duke Orsino
in Twelfth Night, to appear
languid and lovesick for
ladies they hardly knew.
This miniature shows one
such romantically-inclined
young man.

The events of the play *Twelfth Night* do not take place on Twelfth Night, but there is a great deal of merrymaking in the play. Perhaps this is why Shakespeare called the play by this name. However, he also gave it another name – *What You Will*. It is as if he were saying to the audience, 'If you don't like the title of this play, call it whatever you want to!' And later, people did just that by calling it *Malvolio*. Shakespeare seems to suggest that the name of the play is not very important. Two of his other plays, *As You Like It* and *Much Ado About Nothing*, are also named in this casual way.

When the play was written

Almost everyone agrees that the play was written sometime in 1601. This is because, in the play, Shakespeare refers to events which happened in or just before that year. A law student, John Manningham, who was studying in the Middle Temple in London, described a special performance of the play in his diary. This took place in the hall of the Middle Temple, and the occasion was a particular feast to which students were invited in February 1602. Manningham remarks that it was much like another of Shakespeare's plays, *The Comedy of Errors*, which was also about mistaken identities.

Many noblemen joined the Queen's entourage at an early age as page boys, like Viola in Twelfth Night. *These pages clearly found it an enjoyable life.*

A Twelfth Night performance before the Queen

Shakespeare's company performed before Elizabeth I in her palace at Whitehall in the new year of 1601. The Queen's guest of honour on that occasion was an Italian nobleman, Don Virginio Orsino, Duke of Bracciano. He was a young man, aged 28, who was well known for his bravery and courtly manners. He wrote home to his wife that he was entertained by a comedy with songs and dances in it.

Nobody knows what play was performed on that night –

or even if it was one of Shakespeare's. In fact, it is possible that Shakespeare was not the playwright, but one of the actors who played before the Queen and her guest. If this was so, Shakespeare was probably impressed by the handsome young man. To compliment both the Queen and her guest, he named the Duke in his new play 'Orsino' and called the play itself *Twelfth Night*.

We can imagine that Viola, dressed as Cesario in Twelfth Night, *looked just like this girl in 16th-century page's costume depicted by the Italian artist, Giovanni Battista Tiepolo.*

Shakespeare's story

Shakespeare hardly ever invented the stories of his plays. Like other writers at that time, he borrowed them from old stories or poems, but rewrote them in his own words. The plot of *Twelfth Night* was probably borrowed from an Italian play called *Gli Ingannati* (The Deceived Ones), although there were many other stories of girls dressed up as boys in those days. Another tale he may have borrowed from was an English version of the Italian play written by Barnaby Riche and published in 1581.

Girls disguised as boys

Shakespeare uses girls disguised as boys in a number of his plays. *As You Like It* is one and *The Merchant of Venice* is another. One reason why Shakespeare wrote this kind of story was that in those days, all female roles were played by boys. Women were forbidden by law to act on the stage. Boy actors probably felt more at ease on stage when dressed as boys – and the audience, too, would have found it more convincing.

A remote setting

'What country, friends, is this?' asks Viola after her rescue from the shipwreck. 'This is Illyria, lady,' replies the sea captain. Illyria was the ancient name for the country now known as Yugoslavia. Shakespeare often chose to set his

11

plays in faraway places. *A Midsummer Night's Dream*, for example, is set in Greece. It is unlikely that Shakespeare ever visited these places. He probably used these remote settings simply to create a mood – to take the audience away from the real world, and carry them off to a fairy-tale land where all sorts of strange and wonderful things can happen.

Who ever loved, that loved not at first sight?

These words were written by Shakespeare's friend, the poet and playwright, Christopher Marlowe, but they could easily have inspired this play. Viola falls in love with Orsino soon after she meets him. Olivia falls in love with Cesario when she has only seen him once.

Sebastian falls instantly for Olivia, and Orsino for Viola as soon as her identity is revealed. Malvolio falls madly in love with Olivia the moment he is led to believe that she loves him. Perhaps Sir Toby and Maria are the only lovers who have actually had a chance to get to know each other.

Shakespeare pokes gentle fun at nearly all the characters in this play for their attitude to love. Only Viola's secret, unrequited love for Orsino is genuine. The Duke himself is

Through the ages, Shakespeare's plays have provided inspiration for many artists. This depiction of Orsino and Viola in Twelfth Night *is by the 19th century painter, Frederick Richard Pickersgill.*

merely in love with the idea of love. He moans and groans at the pain of his unrequited love, but instantly forgets the object of it when he really does fall in love.

Orsino's pretence of true love would have been well understood by Shakespeare's audience. It was fashionable for young men to worship ladies from afar in those days. Not knowing the ladies personally, they could not possibly have genuine feelings for them. They had to 'create' the feelings in the hope of finding enough favour to get a little closer.

The story of Twelfth Night

> If music be the food of love, play on,
> Give me excess of it, that, surfeiting,
> The appetite may sicken, and so die.
> That strain again, it had a dying fall:
> O, it came o'er my ear like the sweet sound
> That breathes upon a bank of violets,
> Stealing and giving odour. Enough, no more;
> 'Tis not so sweet now as it was before.
>
> Act I Sc i

Orsino, Duke of Illyria, listens to music and talks about love. He is melancholy because he is in love with a noble lady, Countess Olivia, but she has rejected his love. She is determined not to marry because she is in mourning after the death of her beloved brother.

A shipwreck

Meanwhile on the coast of Illyria, a young girl, Viola, has been shipwrecked with the ship's captain and some sailors. She fears that her twin brother, Sebastian, has been drowned. The captain comforts her, saying he believes Sebastian may have survived. He tells Viola about the Duke's love for Olivia, and how Olivia will not receive any visitors or messages because she is in mourning. Viola realizes that it is not possible for her to become one of Olivia's ladies-in-waiting, as she had planned. So instead, she decides to dress as a pageboy and join Orsino's household; she knows that he is fond of music and she can sing and play musical instruments.

Introducing Sir Toby Belch

Olivia has an older cousin, Sir Toby Belch, who lives in her household. He likes to spend his time drinking and

15

merrymaking. But with Olivia now in seclusion, he complains to Maria, Olivia's lady-in-waiting, that this restricts his fun. Sir Toby has a particular friend, Sir Andrew Aguecheek, whom he invites to stay. Sir Andrew is a simple, foolish fellow, and Sir Toby teases him. He tells him that – with Sir Toby's help – he can win Olivia's hand in marriage. He encourages Sir Andrew to show off his talents as a dancer.

Sir Toby urging Sir Andrew to dance
No, Sir, it is legs and thighs. Let me see thee caper. Ha, higher! Ha, ha, excellent!

Act i Sc iii

Viola becomes the page Cesario

After only a few days in the Duke's court, Viola has won Orsino's confidence, and she has fallen in love with him. He knows her as the pageboy called Cesario and sends her to bear messages of his love to Olivia. She agrees to do so but with reluctance because of her own love for the Duke.

Olivia with her household

Among Olivia's servants is the Clown, Feste. Because she is in mourning, Olivia has little patience for Feste's efforts to amuse her. The steward of her household is Malvolio. He is serious and self-important. He dislikes frivolity of any kind, so he disapproves of the Clown – and even more of Sir Toby and Sir Andrew.

When Maria announces that there is a young man at the gate, Malvolio is sent to deal with him. But Malvolio returns to say that the youth insists on seeing Olivia. According to Malvolio, he is 'well favoured' and this arouses Olivia's curiosity. Putting on her mourning veil, she agrees to see him.

Viola disguised as Cesario has prepared her speech and asks Olivia to draw her veil so that she can see her face. When she does, Viola is struck by Olivia's beauty and declares she should not keep it hidden from the world. Olivia replies with a joke, saying she will leave a copy of it in her will.

Olivia on her beauty
. . I will give out divers schedules of my beauty. It shall be inventoried, and every particle and utensil labelled to my will. As, item, two lips indifferent red; item, two grey eyes, with lids to them; item, one neck, one chin, and so forth.

Act I Sc v

Olivia says that she cannot return Orsino's love. Then Viola declares what *she* would do if she were as deeply in love as Orsino is with Olivia.

How Viola would woo a lover
Make me a willow cabin at your gate,
And call upon my soul within the house;
Write loyal cantons of contemned love,
And sing them loud even in the dead of night;
Halloo your name to the reverberate hills,
And make the babbling gossip of the air
Cry out 'Olivia!' O, you should not rest
Between the elements of air and earth,
But you should pity me.

Act I Sc v

Olivia is touched by this speech but again says she cannot love Orsino. She urges Cesario to return to see her, and when he leaves, she realises she has fallen in love with the page. Pretending that he has left a ring behind, she sends Malvolio after him, asking him to return the following day.

Sebastian is alive

By good luck Viola's twin brother, Sebastian, has survived the shipwreck. He was rescued by Antonio, a sea captain. Sebastian thinks Viola is probably dead but he wants to go to Orsino's court. Antonio, who is in trouble with the authorities in Illyria, reluctantly agrees to go with him. Meanwhile, Malvolio has delivered the ring to Viola. She realises that Olivia has fallen in love with 'Cesario'. Somehow she must solve this problem; everything has become too complicated. Viola has fallen in love with Orsino but he is in love with Olivia. Olivia is in love with Cesario – who is Viola disguised as a boy!

A night of merrymaking

Back in Olivia's house, Sir Toby, Sir Andrew and the Clown are enjoying a jolly evening drinking and talking. Just after the Clown has entertained the company with a love song, Maria arrives. It is well after midnight and she complains about the noise. Olivia has been disturbed and has sent Malvolio to put a stop to the celebrations.

Feste's love song

O mistress mine, where are you roaming?
O stay and hear, your true love's coming,
*   That can sing both high and low.*
Trip no further, pretty sweeting:
Journeys end in lovers meeting,
*   Every wise man's son doth know.*

What is love? 'tis not hereafter,
Present mirth hath present laughter;
*   What's to come is still unsure:*
In delay there lies no plenty;
Then come kiss me, sweet and twenty,
*   Youth's a stuff will not endure.*

Act II Sc iii

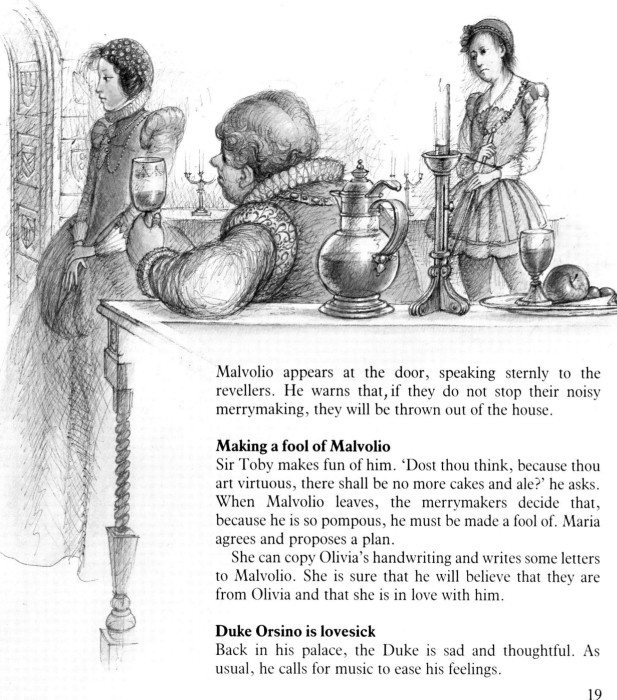

Malvolio appears at the door, speaking sternly to the revellers. He warns that, if they do not stop their noisy merrymaking, they will be thrown out of the house.

Making a fool of Malvolio

Sir Toby makes fun of him. 'Dost thou think, because thou art virtuous, there shall be no more cakes and ale?' he asks. When Malvolio leaves, the merrymakers decide that, because he is so pompous, he must be made a fool of. Maria agrees and proposes a plan.

She can copy Olivia's handwriting and writes some letters to Malvolio. She is sure that he will believe that they are from Olivia and that she is in love with him.

Duke Orsino is lovesick

Back in his palace, the Duke is sad and thoughtful. As usual, he calls for music to ease his feelings.

As the court musicians play, Orsino talks to his page about love, saying how much suffering it causes.

Orsino calls for music

Give me some music. Now good morrow, friends.
Now, good Cesario, but that piece of song,
That old and antique song we heard last night;
Methought it did relieve my passion much,
More than light airs and recollected terms
Of these most brisk and giddy-paced times . . .

Mark it, Cesario, it is old and plain;
The spinsters and the knitters in the sun,
And the free maids that weave their thread with bones
Do use to chant it; it is silly sooth,
And dallies with the innocence of love,
Like the old age.

Act II Sc iv

Orsino is surprised when Viola talks herself with such feeling about love. But he advises that a youth should not marry an older woman.

Orsino's advice

. . . Let still the woman take
An elder than herself, so wears she to him,
So sways she level in her husband's heart:
For, boy, however we do praise ourselves,
Our fancies are more giddy and unfirm,
More longing, wavering, sooner lost and worn,
Than women's are.

Act II Sc iv

Viola tells him of a woman's constancy in love; she is, of course, expressing her own feelings although the Duke does not know this.

20

Orsino on the sufferings of love

Come hither, boy. If ever thou shalt love,
In the sweet pangs of it remember me:
For such as I am, all true lovers are,
Unstaid and skittish in all motions else,
Save in the constant image of the creature
That is belov'd.

Act II Sc iv

21

How Malvolio is tricked

Maria has hidden the letters in a spot where she knows Malvolio will find them. Then she – with Sir Toby and Sir Andrew – hide in a box tree to watch what happens. Just as planned, Malvolio finds the letters and proudly believes that they are a secret confession of Olivia's love for him. Following the instructions in the letters, he goes off to don yellow stockings with cross garters.

> **What Malvolio reads**
> *Some are born great, some achieve greatness, and some have greatness thrust upon them.*
>
> Act II Sc v

Viola now goes off to see Olivia, as she promised the Duke she would. But this meeting becomes very awkward when Olivia confesses her love for Cesario. Viola departs as quickly as she can.

A duel is planned

In order to egg Sir Andrew on in his wooing of Olivia, Sir Toby and Fabian, another member of Olivia's household, suggest that he challenge Cesario to a duel. Just at that moment, Maria announces that Malvolio has been seen – in yellow stockings, cross-gartered and with a silly smile.

22

Malvolio's 'very strange manner'

When Olivia sees Malvolio, she is surprised at his appearance – and even more so when he calls her 'sweetheart'. She thinks he is suffering from midsummer madness and tells Maria and Sir Toby to take care of him. They, however, tease him more and lock him away.

Meanwhile Sir Andrew has written a letter challenging Viola to a duel. Sir Toby tells Viola and Sir Andrew, separately, how skilful their opponent is with a sword. In fact, neither is at all brave or skilful!

Sebastian and Antonio in Illyria

While all this has been going on, Sebastian has made his way to the main town in Illyria. His friend, Antonio, has followed in secret because he is wanted by the police. He gives Sebastian some money to explore the city, arranging to meet him later at an inn.

How the duel is stopped

Both Sir Andrew and Viola are terrified of fighting the duel, but urged on by Sir Toby and Fabian they draw swords. Just then, Antonio appears and leaps to Viola's defence. But, alas, the officers of the law have spotted him and he is immediately arrested. Because they are identical twins, Antonio thinks Viola is Sebastian, so he is surprised and angry when Viola cannot give him money.

Love at first sight

Meanwhile, a confused Sebastian has been taken by the Clown to see Olivia. The moment he meets Olivia, he falls in love with her. As if in a dream, he readily agrees to become betrothed to her. She, of course, thinks he is Cesario.

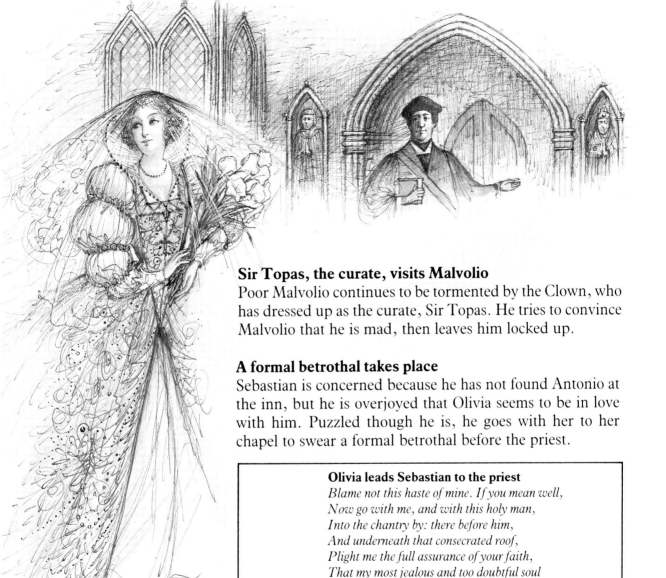

Sir Topas, the curate, visits Malvolio

Poor Malvolio continues to be tormented by the Clown, who has dressed up as the curate, Sir Topas. He tries to convince Malvolio that he is mad, then leaves him locked up.

A formal betrothal takes place

Sebastian is concerned because he has not found Antonio at the inn, but he is overjoyed that Olivia seems to be in love with him. Puzzled though he is, he goes with her to her chapel to swear a formal betrothal before the priest.

> **Olivia leads Sebastian to the priest**
> *Blame not this haste of mine. If you mean well,*
> *Now go with me, and with this holy man,*
> *Into the chantry by: there before him,*
> *And underneath that consecrated roof,*
> *Plight me the full assurance of your faith,*
> *That my most jealous and too doubtful soul*
> *May live at peace.*
>
> Act IV Sc iii

Mistaken identity

Orsino, with Viola, arrives at Olivia's house to court her in person but just then, Antonio and the law officers appear.

25

Viola points out to the Duke that Antonio was the man who rescued her in the duel. But the sea captain turns on her, calling her ungrateful.

When Olivia appears, there is even more confusion. She tells the Duke that she must reject his love because 'Cesario' is her betrothed. Viola, alarmed, declares she must follow Orsino.

> **Viola follows the Duke**
> . . . *After him I love*
> *More than I love these eyes, more than my life,*
> *More, by all mores, than e'er I shall love wife.*   Act v Sc i

The priest arrives and confirms Olivia's story. With this, the Duke orders Viola out of his sight; she has betrayed him.

Just at that moment Sir Toby and Sir Andrew appear, followed by Sebastian. Everyone sees at once how similar the two young people are. Sebastian speaks lovingly to Olivia and greets Antonio with affection. Viola is overjoyed to see Sebastian, the twin brother she feared dead. She reveals that she is disguised.

A double wedding is planned

When Orsino realises that the page he has grown so fond of is a girl, he at once decides to marry her. Olivia, pleased that the mix-up is sorted out, suggests a double wedding.

Olivia orders that Malvolio be released and brought before her. She recognises Maria's handwriting on the letters and explains to Malvolio how he has been tricked. His pride and vanity have been deeply hurt and he vows revenge – on Maria and Sir Toby (who, it seems, have also just married). He storms out leaving the Clown to sing the last words of the play.

The Clown's song

When that I was and a little tiny boy,
With hey, ho, the wind and the rain,
A foolish thing was but a toy,
For the rain it raineth every day.

But when I came to man's estate,
With hey, ho, the wind and the rain,
'Gainst knaves and thieves men shut their gates,
For the rain it raineth every day.

Act v Sc i

27

The play's characters

Viola

Orsino

Sebastian on Viola

. . . *she bore a mind that envy
could not but call fair.*

Act II Sc i

Viola

Viola is one of Shakespeare's most charming heroines. She is not only beautiful and accomplished, she is also practical and courageous. When she believes her brother is dead, she does not bemoan her fate or go into mourning like Olivia. Instead, she goes out to seek employment. She falls in love with the Duke, but loyally tries to win Olivia for him, keeping her own real love secret. When she tells Orsino how constant and enduring a woman's love can be, we know she means it.

Orsino

A noble duke, in nature as in name

The Duke is young but rather moody. He is in love with the idea of love. His love for Olivia is unlike the real affection he feels for Viola. He is a cultured man and loves music. Everyone, including Olivia, has a good opinion of him. When he proposes to Viola, we feel sure they will make a happy couple.

Olivia

Olivia is a beautiful countess. Although young, she is a capable and determined woman. At first she grieves too much for her brother, but when she falls in love with Cesario, she is keen to marry him quickly. She is generous not only to Sir Toby but also to Malvolio, and she runs her household well. She firmly refuses Orsino's love but adapts herself, when she falls in love, to changed circumstances.

Sir Andrew Aguecheek

I knew 'twas I for many call me fool

Sir Andrew is a true comic character. He is silly, cowardly and never suspects that he is being used and tricked by Sir Toby. He enjoys merrymaking with Sir Toby and has no great ambition in life. When Sir Toby asks him, 'Does not life consist of the four elements?' he replies, 'I think rather it consists of eating and drinking.'

Sir Toby Belch

I am sure care's an enemy of life.

Sir Toby is intent on enjoying himself, usually at other people's expense. Even though he is a bully, a cheat and a drunkard, he is a likeable rogue who is always cheerful. When he marries the quick-witted and practical Maria, they are a well-matched pair.

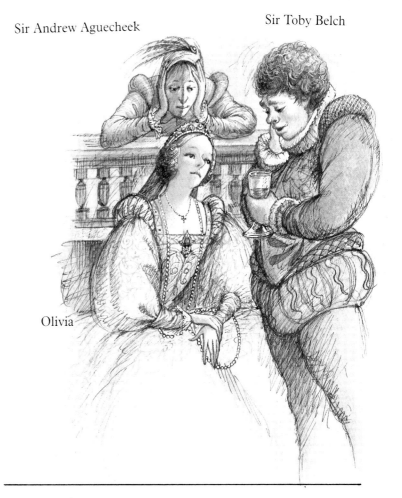

Sir Andrew Aguecheek

Sir Toby Belch

Olivia

Olivia criticises Malvolio

O, you are sick of self-love, Malvolio, and taste with a distempered appetite. To be generous, guiltless, and of free disposition, to take those things for bird-bolts that you deem cannon-bullets.

Act I Sc v

29

Malvolio

Feste, the Clown

Malvolio

Malvolio is one of Shakespeare's most famous characters, whom everyone laughs at because he is so pompous and vain. Yet he is a loyal servant to Olivia who is anxious not to lose him. Although Shakespeare makes fun of him, he is dignified and full of courage when defending himself against the Clown. He has been unfairly tricked and, like Olivia, we feel that he has been 'most notoriously abused.'

Feste, the Clown

He must observe their mood on whom he jests,
The quality of persons, and the time:
. . .This is a practice
As full of labour as a wise man's art.

In Tudor times, many princes and noblemen employed a jester or clown. Generally, they were witty, amusing and able to sing and dance, just as Feste does. Often they wore brightly coloured costumes, and a cap with bells attached to it. Feste is not a 'natural' fool as Sir Andrew is, but a clever man who can out-talk everyone and win arguments. He enjoys the company of Maria, Sir Toby and Sir Andrew, and sings cheerful songs for them. When with the Duke, he matches his mood by singing melancholy songs.

Feste's 'old and antique song'

Come away, come away, death,
And in sad cypress let me be laid.
Fly away, fly away breath,
I am slain by a fair cruel maid:
My shroud of white, stuck all with yew
O prepare it.

Act II Sc iv

The life and plays of Shakespeare

Life of Shakespeare

1564 William Shakespeare born at Stratford-upon-Avon.

1582 Shakespeare marries Anne Hathaway, eight years his senior.

1583 Shakespeare's daughter, Susanna, is born.

1585 The twins, Hamnet and Judith, are born.

1587 Shakespeare goes to London.

1591-2 Shakespeare writes *The Comedy of Errors*. He is becoming well-known as an actor and writer.

1592 Theatres closed because of plague.

1593-4 Shakespeare writes *Titus Andronicus* and *The Taming of the Shrew*: he is member of the theatrical company, the Chamberlain's Men.

1594-5 Shakespeare writes *Romeo and Juliet*.

1595 Shakespeare writes *A Midsummer Night's Dream*.

1595-6 Shakespeare writes *Richard II*.

1596 Shakespeare's son, Hamnet, dies. He writes *King John* and *The Merchant of Venice*.

1597 Shakespeare buys New Place in Stratford.

1597-8 Shakespeare writes *Henry IV*.

1599 Shakespeare's theatre company opens the Globe Theatre.

1599-1600 Shakespeare writes *As You Like It*, *Henry V* and *Twelfth Night*.

1600-01 Shakespeare writes *Hamlet*.

1602-03 Shakespeare writes *All's Well That Ends Well*.

1603 Elizabeth I dies. James I becomes king. Theatres closed because of plague.

1603-04 Shakespeare writes *Othello*.

1605 Theatres closed because of plague.

1605-06 Shakespeare writes *Macbeth* and *King Lear*.

1606-07 Shakespeare writes *Antony and Cleopatra*.

1607 Susanna Shakespeare marries Dr John Hall. Theatres closed because of plague.

1608 Shakespeare's granddaughter, Elizabeth Hall, is born.

1609 *Sonnets* published. Theatres closed because of plague.

1610 Theatres closed because of plague. Shakespeare gives up his London lodgings and retires to Stratford.

1611-12 Shakespeare writes *The Tempest*.

1613 Globe Theatre burns to the ground during a performance of Henry VIII.

1616 Shakespeare dies on 23 April.

Shakespeare's plays

The Comedy of Errors
Love's Labour's Lost
Henry VI Part 2
Henry VI Part 3
Henry VI Part 1
Richard III
Titus Andronicus
The Taming of the Shrew
The Two Gentlemen of Verona
Romeo and Juliet
Richard II
A Midsummer Night's Dream
King John
The Merchant of Venice
Henry IV Part 1
Henry IV Part 2
Much Ado About Nothing
Henry V
Julius Caesar
As You Like It
Twelfth Night
Hamlet
The Merry Wives of Windsor
Troilus and Cressida
All's Well That Ends Well
Othello
Measure for Measure
King Lear
Macbeth
Antony and Cleopatra
Timon of Athens
Coriolanus
Pericles
Cymbeline
The Winter's Tale
The Tempest
Henry VIII

Index

Numerals in *italics* refer to picture captions.

Acknowledgements
The publishers would like to thank Morag Gibson and Patrick Rudd for their help in producing this book.

Picture credits
p.1 Governors of Royal Shakespeare Theatre, p.3 Victoria & Albert Museum (photo Bridgeman Art Library), p.5 Fitzwilliam Museum, Cambridge, p.7, 8 Victoria & Albert Museum (photos Bridgeman Art Library), p.12 John B. Freeman & Co, p.11 Roy Miles Fine Paintings (photo Bridgeman Art Library), p.13 Sotheby's, London (photo Bridgeman Art Library).